Blind Dog Soots

Written by John Parsons
Illustrated by Margaret Power

Contents

NELSON
CENGAGE Learning™
For learning solutions, visit **cengage.com.au**

Meet the Characters

The Narrator

The boy who tells the story about his dog.

Seth

The narrator's older brother.

Soots

A blind dog.

Dear Reader

I have a little blind dog and it just so happens that his name is Soots. Even though he can't see, he is a brave dog and has plenty of adventures. He has an amazing memory to help him get around. He also uses his hearing and his sense of smell and touch to find his way. He's the inspiration for this story – I hope you enjoy it!

John Parsons
Author

Behind the House

1. The house
2. The old mine shaft
3. The way out

1 Prologue

In Nightingale, everything was connected to the coalmine.

Everybody had a parent who worked there. Everybody's house was owned by the mine. Everywhere you looked, there were mining trucks and machinery; and whatever you ran your finger over, there was a thin coating of coal dust. Everyone expected that when my brother, Seth, and I left school, we'd probably work at the coalmine, too.

It was natural, therefore, that our dog was called Soots. It also helped that his fur was as black as the coal that Nightingale depended on.

Soots had been our dog for about eleven years before Seth and I noticed something wrong. He started bumping into things and

lost sight of the sticks we threw for him. Dr Valentine, the town's vet, told us that it was common for old dogs like Soots to slowly go blind.

That was sad. But Dr Valentine said if we kept looking after him and made sure we didn't change too much in the house, Soots would be just fine. Dr Valentine said dogs have an amazing sense of where they are, even if they can't see. Dogs keep a map of what they touch and smell in their heads.

At the time, we thought that was pretty amazing. Little did we know, our little blind dog, Soots, would one day save our lives.

2 A Dog In Trouble

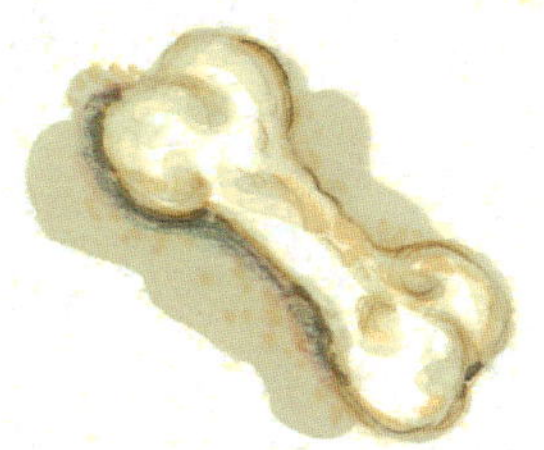

Soots was a terrier. That meant he loved to dig. Whenever he got his teeth into a big old bone from Mum's soup-pot, he never gnawed at it like other dogs. He used to trot away with the bone hanging from his jaws and bury it somewhere. In fact, I can't ever remember seeing Soots chew on a bone – he liked to hide his stash of takeaways in a secret place that no-one else knew about.

The other thing terriers love is chasing other animals – especially rabbits. And that's where our adventure started, on the first day of the summer holidays.

The first I knew of it was when I heard a volley of furious barks from outside our back porch. I raced outside just in time to see Soots and a rabbit tearing through the long grass in the paddock behind our house.

"Soots!" I yelled. "Come back!" But it was no good. He had the scent of that rabbit and nothing was going to stop him, whether he could see or not!

I knew I'd have to go after him, otherwise he'd take forever to find his way home. With a rabbit on his mind, there was no way Soots was going to give up before nightfall. I was a little bit worried because Seth and I had been told never to go into the paddock without an adult. When you live in a coal mining town, you know that there are old mine shafts all over the place, and you better stick to the roads and paths, unless you want to break a leg – or worse.

As I was debating whether to climb over the fence, something suddenly made up my mind for me. Soots's barks were no longer excited and breathless. I heard a loud yelp and then there was nothing.

I knew my dog was in trouble. My heart sank. What had happened?

I leapt over the fence like a runner in a hurdles race, trying to follow the swathe through the long grass where Soots had been chasing the rabbit.

"Soots!" I called. "Soots!" There was no answer.

I stopped in the middle of the paddock, straining my ears for a sound. Apart from the distant noise from the mine, there was only the swish of the wind in the long grass. Soots had quite simply disappeared.

3 Look Out!

I ran back to the house, yelling for my brother Seth to come quickly. He poked his head out of the upstairs bedroom window when he heard me.

"What's up?" he called.

"Soots is missing," I panted. "We need to find him."

Seth was downstairs in a flash. I quickly explained what happened. Seth and I climbed back over the fence and headed off into the long grass.

We called and we searched and we whistled but … nothing.

Until, after about half an hour …

"What was that?" I called. Seth stopped dead in his tracks, and we both shut our eyes, concentrating on any sound we could hear.

And then I heard it again. A faint, distant yelping.

I whirled around and darted towards the sound, closely followed by Seth. It was just as well, because it was only his quick thinking that saved me.

I didn't see it.

"Look out!" he cried. I stopped dead, but it was too late. I hadn't seen the menacing blackness at my feet and suddenly I felt the ground crumbling. It was as if the earth was sucking me down into the darkness.

A split second later, Seth's strong hands grabbed my shirt and hauled me out of the hole. I lay on the grass, gasping for breath, and hoping that Seth didn't notice how much I was shaking.

“That’s some rabbit hole,” I shuddered.

“That’s no rabbit hole. That’s a mine shaft,” said Seth, who was shaking as well. “That was close.”

Then we heard another yelp, a little louder this time. With a mixture of joy and dread, we realised we had found Soots.

“I’ll go and get my torch,” said Seth, racing back towards the house.

“And bring a rope!” I yelled.

I peered into the inky darkness, hoping it wasn’t a vertical shaft. That would mean that Soots would have fallen a long way and could be lying injured at the bottom. I called out to him so he’d know we were close.

When Seth returned with the torch, we could see that the hole led into a steep tunnel.

Seth and I looked at each other, but there was never any question about whether we’d go or not. Soots needed us.

4 Lost!

We crawled into the shaft. Seth went first with his torch, and it wasn't long before that was the only light we could see. We called out to reassure Soots every so often and he'd reply with a bark or a whimper.

After about twenty metres, the shaft widened out until it was big enough to stand up in, if we stooped. It was like a maze. Tunnels went off to the left and the right. There were other shafts in the floor that we gingerly avoided. Seth and I carefully picked our way deeper and deeper into the tunnel. We were tense. We knew we shouldn't have gone into the paddock, let alone down the shaft.

Suddenly, a barrage of anxious barks made us stop in our tracks.

"Soots," I called. "Soots. Where are you?"

That's when things started to go wrong. Horribly wrong.

I should have explained that when Soots went blind, his eyes turned cloudy. It's as if

there were a couple of flat discs right where his pupils used to be.

And when you shone a torch at those discs, instead of the usual green glow, they reflected a weird white colour. And because Soots was black, that's all Seth saw racing towards him in the darkness, like some terrifying wild animal.

He dropped the torch in terror, and it smashed to pieces. There was a flicker … and everything plunged into darkness.

"Seth!" I called into the blackness. I dropped to my knees and crawled to where I'd heard the torch fall. I felt horribly alone. It was darker than any night I'd ever experienced.

With my courage draining away, I inched forward. And suddenly, I bumped into something. It was Seth. A hand grabbed my arm.

And then I felt something licking my face.

We'd found our little blind dog. Or rather, he'd found us!

After we'd hugged, cuddled and patted Soots, and he'd wiggled and licked and whimpered in delight, reality set in.

"What do we do now?" Seth's voice sounded eerie. "We'll never find our way back in the dark."

"We must stay together," I said, trying to sound brave. "As soon as Mum notices we're not around, she'll start looking."

But there's something else I should explain. When you can see absolutely nothing, time seems to stretch forever. A second becomes a minute. A minute becomes an hour. And pretty soon, Seth and I realised we were in deep trouble. Our torch was smashed and useless. No one would ever find us, lost in a forgotten mine shaft. And we'd never find our way out.

I tried to quell the rising feeling of panic in my stomach. And then I heard something unusual.

It was as if Soots was scraping something with his teeth. I felt down until I found his head. He gave me a little lick and returned to his scraping. I felt around some more and I realised what he was doing.

He was gnawing on a bone!

"It's probably from the last kid who got lost in here," said Seth, gloomily.

I knew he was trying to be funny, but I couldn't shake the awful feeling that it might be true.

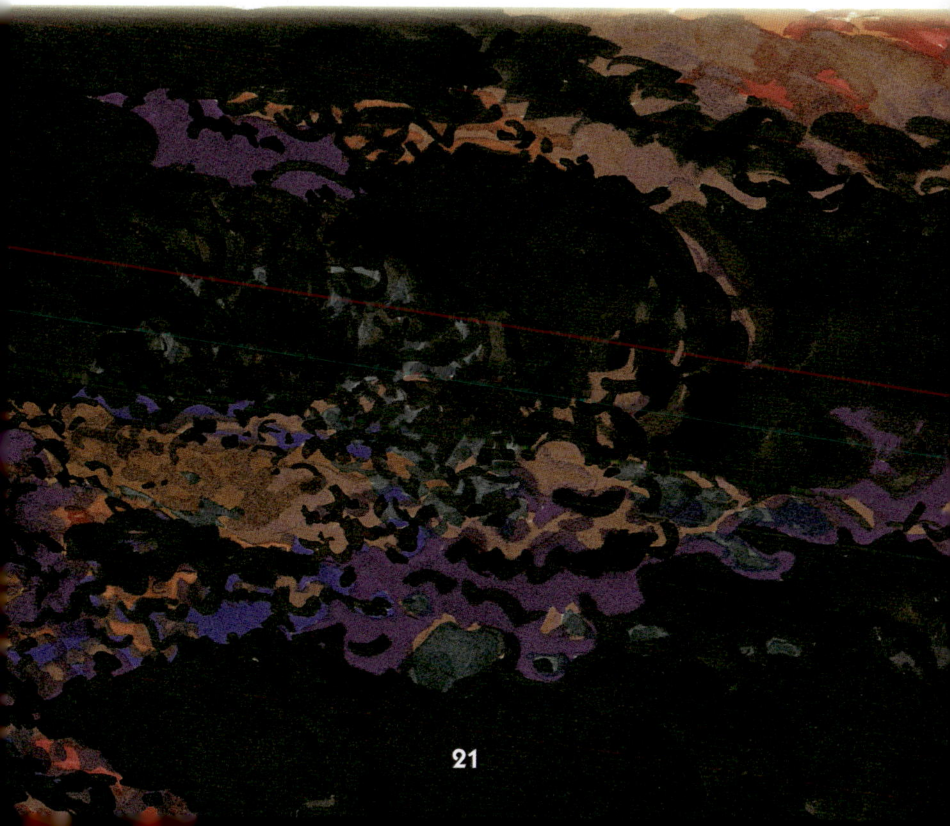

5 Old Bones

After what seemed like hours sitting in the pitch-black cave, Seth and I stopped talking. We listened to each other breathing. We listened to Soots gnawing at his bone. And then we heard him pad cautiously away.

It didn't really matter to Soots whether it was dark or light. To him, it was all the same. He felt his way around and made up a map in his head.

A few seconds later, I heard a dragging sound, like a piece of chalk on a blackboard.

Then he did it again. Finally, he nestled in between Seth and me and started crunching on his bone.

I reached down to tickle his ears, and my hand brushed against the dry bone. But there wasn't just one. There were three.

"One for each of us, huh, Soots?" I said, smiling. "Thanks."

And then I sat bolt upright, as if a flash of lightning had lit up the entire cave!

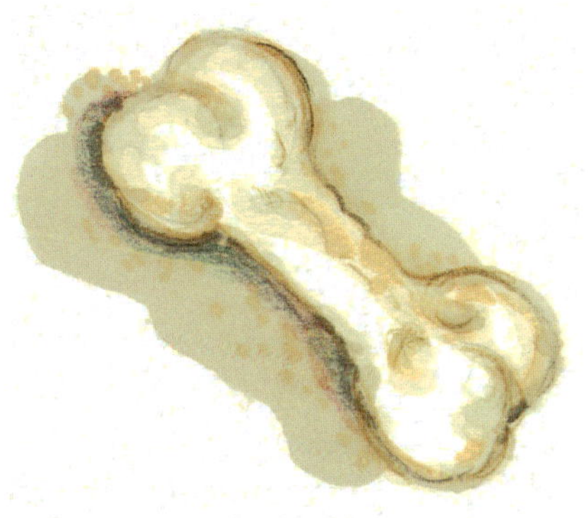

These were Soots's old bones!

If Soots's breath hadn't smelled of rotten old bones, I could have kissed him. He was sharing his stash of soup bones with us!

And that meant one thing! If Soots knew the cave well enough to hide his soup bones, he had to know how to get out as well.

As soon as I explained to Seth what was happening, it was like a surge of electricity ran through us both.

"Soots! Soots!" we cajoled. "Find the bones! Find the bones!"

Soots nuzzled in closer and licked our hands. He was enjoying himself, sharing his secret hideout with us but we were more interested in seeing daylight again.

"Soots, bones," I said. "Take us to the bones."

I felt Soots rise and stretch lazily. He padded off, and Seth and I blindly felt our way after him.

After what seemed like ages, we found a pile of soup bones that would have made litres of beef stock. If I could have seen Soots, I really *would* have kissed him, stinky breath or not.

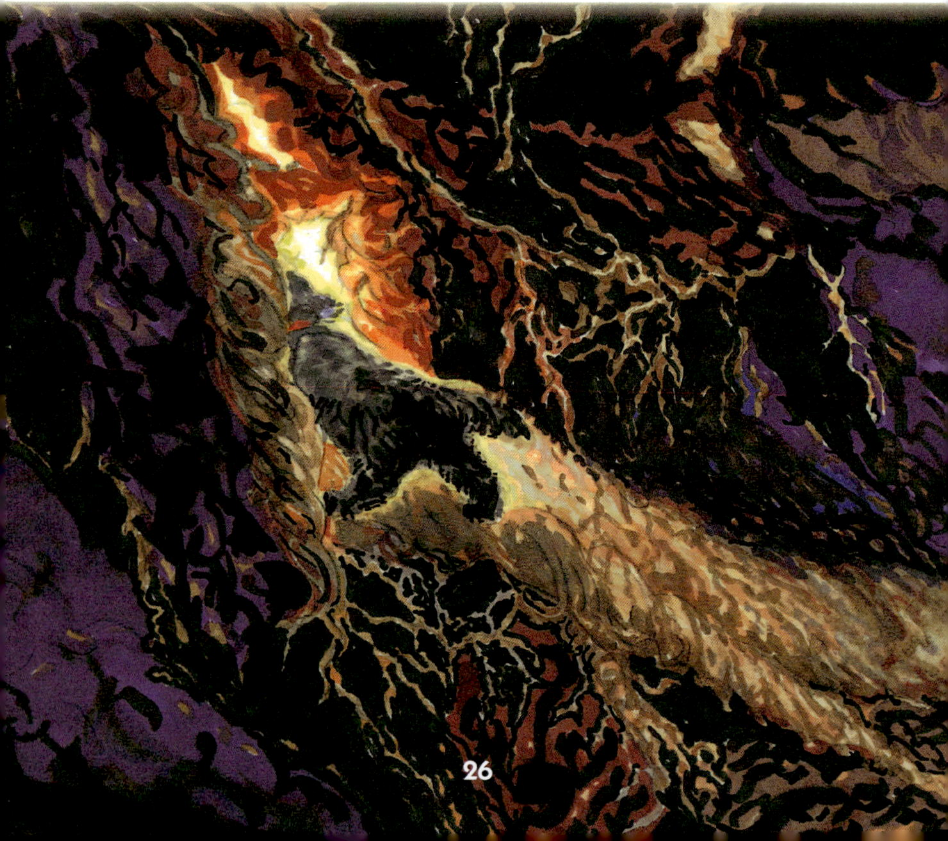

"Good boy," I said. "Now, let's go home."

Soots let out a happy woof and we heard him scrabbling in some dirt ahead of us. We still couldn't see a thing, but we pressed on. Suddenly, a shaft of light streamed down into the darkness.

Seth and I blinked. Soots stretched himself on his belly and finally clambered out between some tree roots. He had a giant grin on his face, as if he'd been delighted to show us where his huge collection of secret bones was.

It took some digging, but as our little blind dog Soots sat on the edge of the shaft, his tail wagging, Seth and I finally extricated ourselves from the old mine tunnel.

6 Epilogue

We were grounded, of course, for an entire week. Getting lost in a disused mine shaft was a sure-fire way to make our parents mad. But we didn't mind. It meant we were able to spend more time with our little dog.

In a lot of ways, it actually brought us even closer. For a few short hours, Seth and I had learnt what it was like for Soots.

It was just like Dr Valentine said. Being blind never troubled Soots, even as he got older and older. We took especially good care of him – and with a good map in his head, he was always able to hide the extra bones that Seth and I slipped him from then on.

THE END

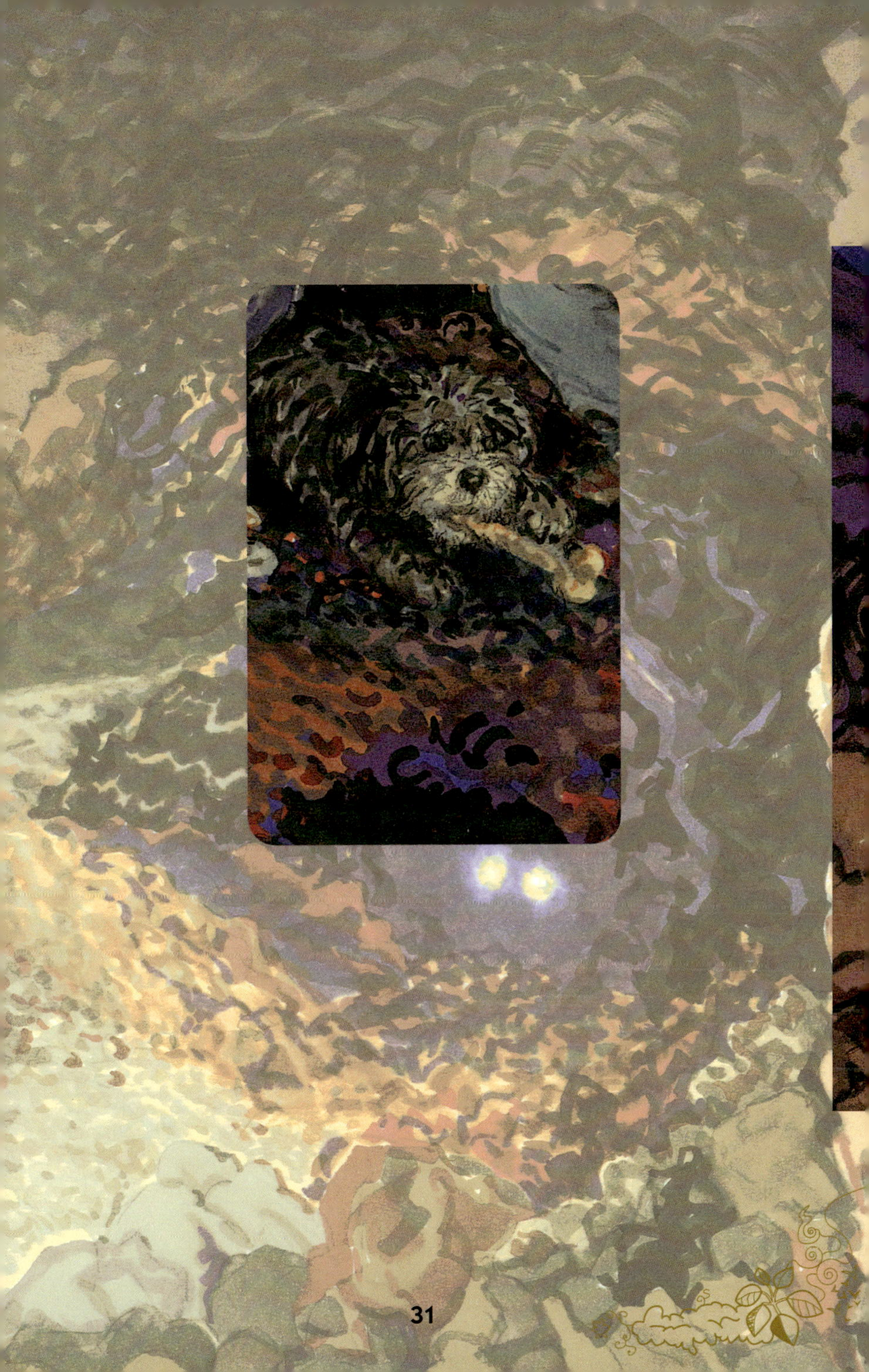

Author's Note

Here's a photo of the *real* Soots, who inspired this story. I thought you'd like to meet him!